City Mouse—Country Mouse

and two more mouse tales from Aesop

City Mouse—Country Mouse

and two more mouse tales from Aesop

Pictures by MARIAN PARRY

SCHOLASTIC BOOK SERVICES NEW YORK · TORONTO · LONDON · AUCKLAND · SYDNEY · TOKYO

ISBN: 0-590-04438-9

Text copyright © 1970 by Scholastic Magazines, Inc. Illustrations copyright © 1970 by Marian Parry. All rights reserved. Published by Scholastic Book Services, a division of Scholastic Magazines, Inc.

16 15 14 13 12 11   0/8

Printed in the U.S.A.

City Mouse—Country Mouse

Once upon a time a City Mouse went to visit
his cousin in the country.

Welcome, Cousin!

The Country Mouse was happy to see his cousin.

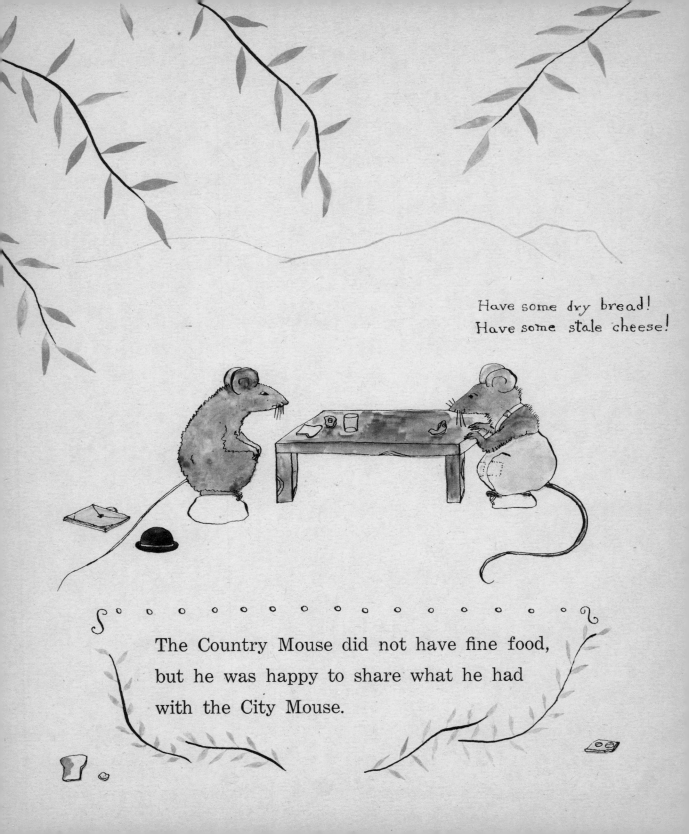

Have some dry bread!
Have some stale cheese!

The Country Mouse did not have fine food,
but he was happy to share what he had
with the City Mouse.

Dear Cousin, how can you
eat such plain food?
Come visit me in the city.
I'll give you a good dinner.

Let's go!

The City Mouse turned up his nose at the country food.
And he invited his cousin to have dinner with him
in the city.

No sooner said than done. The two mice set off
for the city.

At last they came to the home of the City Mouse.
It was very late at night.

You must be hungry
after our long trip.

All this food!?
For us?

The City Mouse led the Country Mouse right into
a grand dining room. The leftovers of a fine feast
were still on the table.

Soon the two mice were eating jam and cake
and all that was nice.

Suddenly they heard growling and barking.

All at once the door flew open, and in came
two huge dogs. Both mice ran for their lives.

What!
Going so soon?

I feel like having some
dry bread and stale cheese
for dinner.

The Country Mouse made up his mind to go back
to the country that very night.

What good is fine food if you can't enjoy it!
It is much better to eat plain food in peace.

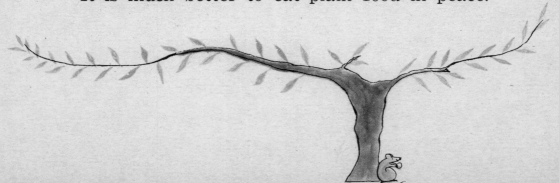

The Lion and the Mouse

Once while a Lion was sleeping, a little Mouse
ran up and down his back.

Soon the Lion woke up. He put his big paw
on the Mouse. He opened his big jaws to swallow him.

The Mouse begged the Lion to let him go.
He promised to help the Lion some day.

The Lion laughed at the thought of a little Mouse
helping a great Lion. But he lifted his paw,
and he let the Mouse go.

Not long after, the Mouse saw the Lion tied to a tree.
The Lion had been trapped by some hunters.

The little Mouse went up to the great Lion
and he gnawed right through the ropes.
Soon the Lion was free.

"Wasn't I right?" said the little Mouse to the Lion.
"Little friends can do great things."

Belling the Cat

Long ago, the mice had a meeting to talk about
their enemy — the Cat. What could they do about her?

Some said this, and some said that. But at last
a young mouse got up and said he had an idea.

We can never
hear her coming.
Isn't that right?

Right   Right
  Right   Right
 Right   Right
     Right

"The Cat moves without making a sound," he said.
"That's why we are always in danger."

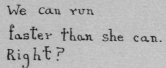

We can run
faster than she can.
Right?

MATCHES

Right   Right
Right
Right   Right   Right

"And," he said, "if we could hear her coming,
it would be easy for us to run away."

"Now — my idea is this. We will tie a bell
around the Cat's neck. Then whenever she moves,
we will hear her. And we can run away!"

Hooray!   Hooray!   Hooray!

Just a minute—

The mice clapped and cheered —
until an old mouse got up and said,

It's easy to think up
a good idea.
But it's not always easy
to make it work.

You and your
big ideas!

"That is all very well. But which one of you
is going to put the bell on the Cat?"
The mice looked at one another in silence.
And no one ever spoke again of belling the Cat.